Dancing Solo

BY JAKE MADDOX

text by Emma Carlson Berne
illustrated by Katie Wood

STONE ARCH
a capstone

Jake Maddox books are published by Stone Arch Books
A Capstone Imprint
1710 Roe Crest Drive
North Mankato, Minnesota 56003
www.capstonepub.com

Library of Congress Cataloging-in-Publication Data
Maddox, Jake, author.
Dancing solo / by Jake Maddox ; text by Emma Carlson Berne ;
illustrated by Katie Wood.
pages cm. -- (Jake Maddox girl sports stories)
Summary: Sarah knows that she is the best dancer in her class, and
she is eager to show off at the upcoming recital — but when a new
move proves unexpectedly difficult and she has to ask for help, her
confidence is shaken.
ISBN 978-1-4342-4142-9 (hardcover) -- ISBN 978-1-4342-7930-9 (pbk.)
-- ISBN 978-1-4342-9286-5 (eBook PDF)
1. Dance--Juvenile fiction. 2. Self-confidence--Juvenile fiction. 3.
Helping behavior--Juvenile fiction. 4. Friendship--Juvenile fiction. [1.
Ballet dancing--Fiction. 2. Self-confidence--Fiction. 3.
Friendship--Fiction.] I. Berne, Emma Carlson, author. II. Wood,
Katie, 1981- illustrator. III. Title.

PZ7.M25643Db 2014
[Fic]--dc23

2013028667

Designer: Alison Thiele
Production Specialist: Charmaine Whitman

Artistic Elements: Shutterstock, 68, 69 (silhouettes)

Printed in China.
092013
007735LEOS14

Table of Contents

CHAPTER ONE

Show-Off

"Up, and plié!" Ms. Rousseau called. Her voice echoed across the large, sunny ballet studio. "Hold please, and then down and finish in second!"

Standing at the barre, Sarah O'Claire rested one hand lightly on the smooth wood. She held her other arm gracefully out to the side. Keeping her heels together, she sank down into her plié. Around her, the rest of the ballerinas pliéd as well.

"Excellent, ladies. Now let's see an arabesque, please," Ms. Rousseau called.

Sarah took her arm off the bar and leaned forward, lifting her right leg behind her into an arabesque. She made sure to keep her toe pointed and her knee straight.

Sarah cast a quick glance around the room. No one else's leg was as straight or as high as hers. And several of the dancers had limp arms. Ms. Rousseau hated that. Sarah smiled to herself and lifted her leg just another inch higher.

"And down! Relax!" the ballet teacher commanded.

The other students dropped their poses with relief, but Sarah made sure she held her arabesque just a few seconds longer. That way everyone could see it.

"Very nice, Sarah!" Ms. Rousseau complimented her.

Across the room, Sarah saw one of the other dancers watching her and rolling her eyes. Sarah tossed her head and looked away. She knew some of the other girls thought she was a show-off.

Well, fine, Sarah thought. *They can think whatever they want. It doesn't change the fact that my arabesque was the best in the class.*

Ms. Rousseau turned off the music and motioned to the dancers. "Girls, gather round please," she called.

When everyone was sitting around her on the floor, Ms. Rousseau pulled out a clipboard. "As many of you know, our annual recital is coming up. We'll be holding tryouts next week," she said.

All the dancers started chattering excitedly. The annual recital was the biggest event at the ballet studio. Their parents came, of course, but so did people from the community and dancers from other schools.

"The theme for this year's recital is fairies in nature," Ms. Rousseau announced. "There will be four lead fairies, one for each season, and several supporting fairies."

Sarah sat up straight and smiled. She knew she'd be cast as one of the leads. There was no doubt about it. And everyone else knew it too.

"The recital will end with all of the fairies in a circle around the Spring Fairy as she dances," Ms. Rousseau said. "That means whoever plays the Spring Fairy will dance a solo."

Sarah tried not to look too eager. But it was clear that the part of the Spring Fairy was meant for her.

"For the auditions, each dancer must dance a three-minute routine," Ms. Rousseau said. "It must include a jeté, an arabesque, which we practiced today, and a pirouette. These are hard steps, especially the pirouette, so you'll all need to practice on your own too."

As soon as Ms. Rousseau finished, the dancers rose to their feet and gathered their bags from the corner of the room.

Sarah slung her own bag over her shoulder. She wasn't worried about the moves Ms. Rousseau had mentioned. She'd already been working on the jeté for months. It'd be easy for her.

On the way out the door, Sarah bumped into Mandy and Alex, two of the other dancers in their class.

"Oops, sorry," Mandy said, smiling at Sarah.

Sarah smiled a little. *Maybe I should be a little friendlier in class,* she thought. *I don't really talk to anyone.*

"Hey, are you guys going to the Spirit Shop for ice cream?" Sarah asked. The dancers often stopped by the Spirit Shop after practice. "We can walk over together."

Mandy and Alex exchanged a quick glance. "Um, actually, we're heading over to Alex's house," Mandy said quickly. "Sorry."

With that, the two girls turned and rushed off down the sidewalk.

Sarah hitched up her dance bag and trudged down the street in the opposite direction.

Whatever, she thought. *Who cares if they don't want to hang out with me. I have to go practice my pirouettes anyway.*

CHAPTER TWO

Harder Than It Looks

Sarah could hardly concentrate during dinner. She was too busy thinking about her upcoming audition. After pushing her chicken and peas around on her plate for several minutes she turned to her mom. "Can I be excused?" she asked.

"You've hardly eaten anything," Mom said.

"I'm not hungry," Sarah replied. "I need to go practice my audition routine."

"Okay, but don't forget about apple pie later!" Mom called up the stairs behind her.

"I don't have time!" Sarah shouted back. "I have to practice!"

Sarah shut her bedroom door behind her and hurried over to the MP3 player sitting in the dock on her dresser. She scrolled through her music and turned on the theme from *Swan Lake*.

Sarah smiled as the music filled the room. *Swan Lake* was her favorite ballet. She always felt inspired when she heard it.

Taking a deep breath, Sarah turned and faced the mirror that took up almost the entire wall. She'd convinced her parents to install it for her last birthday so she could practice. Now she was working on convincing them to install a barre.

Sarah closed her eyes and held her arms out to the side, her feet in second position. She'd already started picturing the routine she wanted to do in her head.

As the music swelled, Sarah did a delicate plié, then ran lightly in a circle using a waltz step, her arms over her head.

Perfect, she thought. *Now, the jeté.*

Sarah increased her speed and leaped into the air, making sure to keep looking forward. She landed gently and moved immediately into the arabesque.

She lifted her leg into the air behind her, making sure to keep her standing leg steady. Then she leaned her upper body slightly forward and held both arms out to the side, feeling her rib cage expand.

No wobbling! she thought firmly.

The music swelled, and Sarah did another jeté, landing with her leg delicately held behind her. Her routine was almost at three minutes, and she still had to do the pirouette, the last required step.

She lifted her back leg and placed it lightly on the inside of her front leg, bent at the knee. Then she used the power of the lift to spin in a circle.

"Oh!" Sarah exclaimed as she suddenly tripped and staggered. She fell against her dresser and bumped the MP3 player. The music stopped.

Sarah shook her head to clear it. *Focus*, she thought sternly.

Sarah started the music again and lifted herself into the pirouette. *Balance, arms out, back straight, and turn —*

"Oof!" Sarah exclaimed as she fell out of position again. This time, she almost fell into the mirror.

Sarah gritted her teeth. "Stop it," she muttered under her breath. "Get it right."

She tried to whirl again and again, but no matter what she did, she kept staggering out of the move.

Sarah sank down on her bed. Her stomach was suddenly fluttering with nerves. *Why can't I do the pirouette?* she thought. *And how am I ever going to play the Spring Fairy if I can't?*

CHAPTER THREE

Making It Look Easy

"Front and one, side and two, back and three . . ." Ms. Rousseau's voice counted out the beats as the dancers stood at the barre the next day.

Sarah moved her foot around to the front, side, and back automatically, but she couldn't stop thinking about the night before. Every time she pictured herself falling against her dresser, her stomach rolled.

Maybe I was just tired, Sarah thought. *There's no reason the pirouette should be such a big deal.*

Ms. Rousseau clapped her hands and turned off the music. "Dancers, move to the center of the room, please," she said. "Let's run through the required steps for the recital auditions. This is your time to ask any questions you may have."

The dancers all hurried to the center of the room and arranged themselves in rows. Sarah took a spot near the back. Usually, she liked to be in the front row so Ms. Rousseau could see how well she was doing, but she was feeling a little shaky after the night before.

Mandy walked over and stood next to her. "Hey," she said, with a small smile.

Sarah glanced over at her. "Hi," she replied. She stared straight ahead at Ms. Rousseau.

"Are you excited for the auditions?" Mandy asked. "I'm kind of nervous. What part are you going to try out for?"

"The Spring Fairy," Sarah said stiffly.

Mandy nodded. "I think I'm just going to try out for one of the supporting fairies," she said. "I don't know if I could dance one of the leads. I'd be so nervous."

Sarah just nodded. She didn't get why Mandy was being so friendly all of a sudden.

"We'll do jetés first," Ms. Rousseau called from the front of the room. "Make sure to give yourself plenty of room. You'll need to run a little in order to jump."

The dancers all spread out, and Ms. Rousseau turned the music back on.

Sarah tried to focus on her own dancing, but she couldn't help watching Mandy out of the corner of her eye. Mandy took a few small running steps, then leaped and landed with a little thud.

That was loud, Sarah thought with satisfaction. She ran and leaped, making sure to launch her body high into the air. She landed back on the floor as lightly as a feather.

After several jetés, Ms. Rousseau changed the music. "Pirouettes now, girls!" she instructed. "Everyone, lift yourself onto your left toe. Now lift your right leg up, keeping your foot flat against the inside of your standing leg, and spin."

Ms. Rousseau moved around the room, adjusting the dancers' arms and legs so everyone was in the proper position.

Sarah tried to focus. She lifted her right leg into the position, held her arms in a circle out in front of her, and tried to spin like Ms. Rousseau had instructed.

But instead of twirling gracefully, Sarah fell out of position. Just like the night before. This time, she almost knocked into Mandy. The other girl looked startled.

"Sorry," Sarah mumbled. She glanced around the room quickly, but no one else seemed to have noticed. The other dancers were busy lifting and spinning effortlessly.

What's wrong with me? Sarah thought. *Why can't I do it?* She'd never had this much trouble with a step before.

Sarah glanced over at Mandy again. She couldn't help noticing that the other girl was performing her pirouette effortlessly.

Sarah scowled. *If she makes it look so easy, why does it feel so hard?* she thought.

CHAPTER FOUR

Stubborn and Solo

After class, the rest of the dancers gathered their things and trickled out of the studio. Sarah waited until everyone else was gone so she could talk to Ms. Rousseau. She had to get the pirouette right, and she didn't want any of the other girls to see her.

"Ms. Rousseau?" Sarah said, walking over to her teacher. "Do you mind if I stay a little later? I want to work on my audition routine some more."

"Of course, Sarah," Ms. Rousseau replied with a smile. "I have to work on a few things in my office. Just holler if you need me."

Sarah nodded, but she knew she wouldn't be asking for help. It was too embarrassing.

I can do it on my own, she thought stubbornly. *I have to.*

The studio seemed strange without the other dancers. It felt so big and empty. Sarah took a deep breath and walked to the center of the room.

Sarah lifted herself up into the starting position for the pirouette. But this time, she didn't even make it to the spin. She wobbled immediately and had to put her other toe down to keep from falling.

Sarah shook her head and tried to focus. She lifted her right foot off the ground and tried to balance. But again, she had to put her foot down to avoid falling over.

This is horrible, Sarah thought. *Now I can't even manage the starting position.*

Sarah tried over and over, but no matter what she did, she kept losing her balance. By the time she finally took a break, her face was red and she was out of breath.

The only sound in the studio was Sarah's heavy breathing. Suddenly, she heard the sound of footsteps across the room.

Sarah gasped and whirled around. Mandy stood there, holding her dance bag in one hand.

"What are you doing here?" Sarah demanded.

Mandy held up the bag. "I forgot this here earlier," she said. She studied Sarah's red, sweaty face and messy hair. "What's up? Are you okay?"

"I'm fine," Sarah snapped. She swiped at her hair. "I'm just getting a little extra practice in before the auditions."

Sarah quickly turned away, pretending to fix her hair in the mirror. She just wanted Mandy to stop looking at her.

Behind her, Mandy cleared her throat. "Um, I know it might not be any of my business," she said, "but I kind of saw you practicing just now. Are you having trouble with the pirouette?"

Sarah stiffened and said nothing. She kept her back turned but watched Mandy in the mirror. Her face was burning with embarrassment.

"I noticed in class too," Mandy continued. "I think your problem might be that —"

"I'm fine!" Sarah snapped, whirling around. She couldn't stand listening to Mandy giving her advice.

I'm the best dancer in the class, Sarah thought. *If anything, I should be giving her advice.*

Sarah took a deep breath and let it out. "I don't need your help," she told Mandy tightly.

Mandy shrugged and backed up a few steps. She held her dance bag in front of her like a shield. "Fine," she replied stiffly. "I was just offering."

With that, Mandy turned on her heel and marched out of the studio.

Sarah stood in the middle of the empty room for a long time after Mandy left. She had a bad feeling that her chance to play the Spring Fairy had just disappeared too.

CHAPTER FIVE

Facing Facts

Sarah hardly slept that night. Every time she closed her eyes, she saw herself stumbling across the stage.

I'm never going to make it through my audition at this rate, Sarah thought. *And forget about playing the Spring Fairy.*

Finally, as the sun was just starting to peek though her curtains, Sarah threw off her covers and sat up in bed. It was no use. She couldn't sleep.

If I can't sleep, I might as well get some practice in, she thought, getting out of bed and pulling on her exercise clothes. *Auditions are only three days away.*

Sarah sat down on the floor in front of the large mirror and laced up her ballet slippers. A feeling of dread settled in the pit of her stomach. Her muscles felt stiff and tense.

She warmed up briefly, then did a few jetés and arabesques to get ready. To her relief, she was able to do them all easily. But Sarah knew she wasn't in the clear yet. If she couldn't do the pirouette, all the jetés in the world wouldn't help her.

Maybe I'm just overthinking it, Sarah thought. *Maybe I just need to throw myself into it.*

Sarah shook out one leg, then the other, trying to convince her stiff muscles to warm up. When she felt a bit looser, she leaned over and turned on her MP3 player. Sarah closed her eyes as the theme from *Swan Lake* filled the air.

Quickly, she ran through the rest of her routine. Plié, then waltz step, jeté, right into an arabesque, then another jeté. Then it was time for the pirouette.

Just do it! Sarah thought.

She lifted her back leg so she was balanced on her other toe and tried to spin quickly. But she lost her balance.

Sarah pitched forward, almost hitting her forehead on the edge of her bedside table. She collapsed onto the floor in a heap.

For a long moment, Sarah sat there silently as the music continued to play. Then she carefully started to untangle her legs and get to her feet.

But as soon as she tried to stand up, Sarah knew something was wrong. A sharp pain shot through her right ankle when she put weight on it.

"Ouch!" Sarah exclaimed, sinking down onto her bed. She grabbed her ankle with both hands, touching it gently as she examined it.

What if I sprained it? Sarah thought nervously.

If her ankle was injured, Sarah knew it wouldn't matter if she could do the pirouette or not. She wouldn't be able to audition.

She carefully flexed her ankle back and forth. The pain seemed to be fading. After a few minutes, she put her foot back on the ground and tried to stand. Her ankle seemed okay.

Sarah breathed a sigh of relief and laid back down on her bed, putting her arm over her eyes. She couldn't keep going like this. She'd almost hurt herself.

There were two choices. She could give up her dream of being the Spring Fairy — or any fairy for that matter.

Or she could ask someone for help. She had to stop pretending like she didn't need it.

Sarah thought about how Mandy had offered to help her. She cringed when she thought of how rude she'd been.

With a sigh, Sarah rolled over and grabbed her cell phone off her bedside table. She ran through the list of dancers' phone numbers. Then she took a deep breath and pressed call.

CHAPTER SIX

Asking for Help

Sarah pulled at her comforter on her bed nervously as she listened to the phone ring. Maybe she'd get lucky and Mandy wouldn't answer. Maybe she was busy. Maybe she was still asleep.

Just then, the ringing stopped. "Hello?" Mandy answered.

Sarah cleared her throat and swallowed hard. "Um, hi, Mandy," she said. "It's Sarah."

Mandy didn't say anything for a long moment. Sarah had a sudden urge to hang up, but she made herself go on.

"So, um, I was just practicing the pirouette in my room," she said.

"Oh, yeah?" Mandy replied. She sounded a little suspicious.

Sarah cleared her throat again. "Yeah," she said. "It's not going very well. In fact, I almost twisted my ankle." She laughed nervously.

"Are you okay?" Mandy asked.

"Yes," Sarah said. "It's just . . . for some reason, I can't quite get this step." The words were hard to say.

"I know," Mandy replied. "That's why I offered to help. But you said no."

Sarah felt her face get hot with embarrassment. All she wanted to do was hang up the phone and forget this conversation had ever happened.

"Yeah, um, I remember," Sarah admitted quietly. "I'm really sorry. I need your help, okay?"

There. She'd said it. The words echoed in her ear. Sarah wondered what she would do if Mandy refused.

"So, why now?" Mandy asked, sounding a little mad. "I mean, you didn't want me to help you yesterday. Now you want my help just because you almost injured yourself?"

"No, that's not it at all!" Sarah insisted. "Well, maybe it's part of the reason. But it's not the whole reason."

She tried to explain. "I've just always been able to do things on my own when it comes to dancing," Sarah said. "It's kind of hard for me to ask for help. But I can see that I need it."

Sarah took a deep breath. "And I'm sorry for turning you down before," she finished. "Really. It was dumb of me."

There was a long silence. Then Mandy sighed. "All right. I get what you're saying," she said. "Meet me in the studio in a couple hours, okay? Ms. Rousseau said it would be open if anyone wanted to practice."

"Okay, great!" Sarah said. "I'll see you there. And thank you!"

Mandy didn't seem to know what to say. "Um, you're welcome," she finally replied before hanging up.

Sarah bounced up from her bed and grabbed her towel for the shower. She didn't feel tired anymore. In fact, she felt more ready than ever to tackle the pirouette.

CHAPTER SEVEN

Mastering the Move

Mandy was already at the studio when Sarah arrived.

"Hi," Sarah said, a little hesitantly, as she put down her bag. She still wasn't at all sure how Mandy felt about her.

But to her relief, Mandy turned toward her with a smile. "Hi," she said.

"It's really nice of you to meet me —" Sarah started to say, but Mandy waved away her words.

"Seriously, it's no big deal, okay?" she replied. Mandy paused, then grinned. "Do you always worry this much?"

Sarah laughed, a little surprised, and nodded. "Yeah, I do. I guess it must be sort of obvious," she said.

Mandy smiled. "Sort of," she agreed. "Anyway, should we get started?" She moved to the center of the room.

Sarah followed. It felt a little weird to have Mandy teaching her. But Sarah didn't care anymore. Mandy seemed pretty nice, and it wasn't exactly like Sarah was doing so great on her own.

Sarah did a few warm-up moves, then turned to Mandy. "So, it's the pirouettes that are just killing me," she said. "You probably already know that."

Mandy nodded. "Yeah, I noticed that the other day. Your jetés are fantastic, by the way," she told Sarah.

Sarah smiled. "Thanks," she said. "But I'm not going to be the Spring Fairy just by doing jetés. Not if I can't do the pirouette too."

"True," Mandy agreed. "Do you want to try to do one? Maybe I'll be able to spot the problem."

"Sure," Sarah agreed with a nod. She did a few waltz steps to get herself into the rhythm, then tried to draw herself into the pirouette. As usual, she managed to get her leg off the ground, but as soon as she started to turn, she lost her balance.

She turned to face Mandy, a little embarrassed.

But Mandy wasn't laughing. Instead, she nodded seriously. "It's basically what I thought the other day," she said. "You're not tracking with your eyes."

"Tracking?" Sarah repeated, looking confused.

"Yeah," Mandy replied. "It's when you fix your eyes on one spot while twirling. Every time you come around, look back at that same spot. Here, I'll show you."

Mandy did a few waltz steps, then lightly stepped into a pirouette. As she began to spin, she whipped her head around so that her eyes kept facing forward throughout the pirouette.

Sarah watched her closely as she twirled. Mandy's form wasn't perfect, but her standing leg was completely solid.

"There," Mandy said. She stopped, a little out of breath. "I always turn my head and keep my eyes on the exit sign. You have to pick a specific place before you start spinning. Then don't take your eyes off it."

"You make it seem so simple," Sarah said. "I've been torturing myself over this."

Mandy shrugged. "You just needed some help. You're a great dancer," she said. "But you can't do the turn without balance."

"That's for sure," Sarah said, nodding. "Okay, let me try."

Sarah stood with one leg extended behind her, the toe delicately touching the floor. She held her arms out in a circle in front of her and glanced around the room, looking for something to focus on. She picked the clock and fixed her eyes on it.

Ignoring the nervous flutter in her stomach, Sarah drew her back leg up and kept her eyes on the clock. Then she used the force of her arms to whirl in a circle.

One turn, there was the clock, then two, she saw the clock again. As Sarah came around the second time, she put her foot down and grinned at Mandy.

"That was awesome!" Mandy cheered.

Sarah had a huge grin on her face. "That's two more turns than I've ever done on my own," she said. "I owe you big time!"

"It looked really good," Mandy said. "You didn't wobble at all. Try it again!"

Sarah got back into position and focused on the clock again. Then she lifted herself onto one toe and began to spin. This time she made it through three turns.

Sarah practiced again and again. Finally, she collapsed on the floor, exhausted. Mandy flopped down beside her.

"I think I've got it. It's not great, but at least I can complete three turns and not fall," Sarah said. "It might not be good enough to get me the Spring Fairy, but at least I can get through the audition without embarrassing myself."

"You're being too hard on yourself," Mandy said. "It looks good."

Sarah turned to look at the other girl. "Thank you," she said, clearing her throat. "Seriously. You didn't have to help me, but you did it anyway." Sarah paused, then went on. "This has been fun."

"Don't worry about it," Mandy told her. "It's been fun for me too."

As they gathered up their things and turned out the lights, Sarah smiled. She'd done more than learn how to do a pirouette today. She'd made a new friend too.

CHAPTER EIGHT

Audition Time

A few days later, Sarah stood next to Mandy at the recital auditions. Mandy was biting her nails nervously as they watched together from the side of the studio.

In the center of the room, Alex was performing her routine. Ms. Rousseau sat in a chair near the front of the room, watching the auditions closely.

"Are you nervous?" Sarah whispered to her new friend.

Mandy nodded in reply. Sarah reached over and squeezed her hand in encouragement.

"You'll do great," Sarah said. "Just take deep breaths, and stay calm. Getting nervous isn't going to help anything."

"Right," Mandy replied. Her voice sounded shaky.

Just then, Ms. Rousseau called, "Mandy Evans, you're up!"

"Good luck!" Sarah whispered as Mandy made her way to the center of the room.

Mandy turned around and smiled. "Thanks," she whispered back.

When Mandy reached the center of the room, she nodded to Ms. Rousseau. The music started, and she began her routine with a series of pliés.

In what seemed like seconds, Mandy was finished. She walked back over to Sarah.

"My timing was off," Mandy complained, shaking her head.

"But your jetés were really high," Sarah replied. "Ms. Rousseau is going to love that."

Just then, Ms. Rousseau called, "Sarah, you're up next."

Mandy smiled at her. "Your turn," she said. "Don't forget to track. You're going to be awesome."

Sarah took a deep breath and made her way to the center of the room. The polished wood surface looked huge spread out before her. She focused on the corner of the window frame across the studio — that's what she would track back to.

"All right, Sarah, whenever you're ready," Ms. Rousseau said.

Sarah nodded, and the music started. She moved first into a gentle plié, then ran in a small circle of waltz steps, keeping her arms held wide. She leaped into her jeté, remembering to turn her head to follow her leading leg, and landed solidly back on the floor.

So far, so good, Sarah thought.

She was starting to relax now. She performed a solid arabesque, followed by a second jeté. Sarah felt her heart pound as she positioned herself for the pirouette.

Sarah glued her eyes to the window frame across the room. Steadying herself, she balanced on one foot and lifted into the pirouette.

Sarah began to spin, whipping her head back around with each rotation so that she stayed focused on the spot she'd chosen. She spun once, then twice, solidly.

As Sarah spun for a third time, her eyes darted away from the window frame for a brief moment, and she wobbled slightly. She caught herself a little clumsily but managed not to fall.

Despite her mistake, Sarah felt calm as the music ended. It hadn't been a perfect audition, but it hadn't been a disaster. And she'd managed to make it through the pirouette . . . with a little help.

Mandy hugged Sarah as she made her way back over to the side of the room. "That was awesome!" she said. "You nailed the pirouette!"

Sarah smiled back at her new friend. "Thanks to you," she said. "I couldn't have done it without you."

* * *

An hour later, the dancers gathered in the hallway as Ms. Rousseau taped a sheet of paper up on the wall. As soon as the list was up, everyone pushed forward to see their parts.

Sarah's heart pounded as she ran her finger down the list until she saw her name.

"Sarah O'Claire, supporting fairy, spring," she read out loud. "Mandy Evans, supporting fairy, winter."

Sarah scrolled back up the list. Alex had landed the role of Spring Fairy.

Sarah turned to face Mandy. "Well, neither of us got leads," she said.

Surprisingly, Sarah realized she wasn't as upset as she would have thought. "But at least we both made it into the recital," she said.

"That's a good way of looking at it," Mandy agreed.

"I probably wouldn't have landed any role if it hadn't been for your help," Sarah said.

"Does that mean maybe we can rehearse together for the recital?" Mandy asked hopefully.

Sarah grinned and put her arm around her new friend. "Absolutely," she said. "Let's start now."

Author Bio

Emma Carlson Berne has written more than a dozen books for children and young adults, including teen romance novels, biographies, and history books. She lives in Cincinnati, Ohio, with her husband, Aaron, her son, Henry, and her dog, Holly.

Illustrator Bio

Katie Wood fell in love with drawing when she was very small. Since graduating from Loughborough University School of Art and Design in 2004, she has been living her dream working as a freelance illustrator. From her studio in Leicester, England, she creates bright and lively illustrations for books and magazines all over the world.

Glossary

ANNUAL (AN-yoo-uhl) — happening once every year or over a period of one year

AUDITION (aw-DISH-uhn) — a short performance by an actor, singer, musician, or dancer to see whether he or she is suitable for a part in a play, concert, etc.

CONCENTRATE (KON-suhn-trate) — to focus your thoughts and attention on something

RECITAL (ri-SYE-tuhl) — a performance by a single performer or by a small group of musicians or dancers

RELIEF (ri-LEEF) — a feeling of freedom from pain or worry

ROUTINE (roo-TEEN) — a regular way or pattern of doing things

STUDIO (STOO-dee-oh) — a room or building in which an artist, photographer, or dancer works

Discussion Questions

1. Why do you think Sarah was so reluctant to ask for help with her dancing? Talk about some possible reasons.

2. Discuss how Sarah and Mandy's relationship changed from the beginning of this story to the end.

3. Do you think Sarah was being a show-off at the start of this story? Talk about your opinion.

Writing Prompts

1. First impressions aren't always right. Write a paragraph about a time your opinion of someone changed from when you first met them.

2. Write about a time in your life that you had to ask for help with something. What was it and who did you ask?

3. Pretend that you are Ms. Rousseau. Who would you choose as the Spring Fairy? Write a paragraph about your choice.

More about Ballet

ARABESQUE indicates a position of the body where a dancer stands on one leg with the supporting leg and foot either *en pointe*, *demi pointe*, or on a flat foot. The back leg may either touch the floor in *tendu* back or be raised at an angle.

JETÉ is a ballet jump or leap during which a dancer transfers his or her weight from one foot to the other; the dancer throws one leg to the front, side, or back and holds the other leg in position while landing.

PLIÉ means "to bend" and is a move done when a dancer smoothly and continuously bends his or her knees. This can be *grand-plié,* which is a bend to the deepest position, or a *demi-plié,* in which a dancer bends his or her knees until just below the hips while staying turned out at the joints, keeping the thighs and knees directly above the toes. The goal is to keep the heels on the ground as long as possible.

PIROUETTE is French for "to turn" and is a move done on one leg, starting with one or both legs in *plié*. Male ballet dancers typically rise up into *relevé* while female dancers rise into *pointe* before turning on one leg.

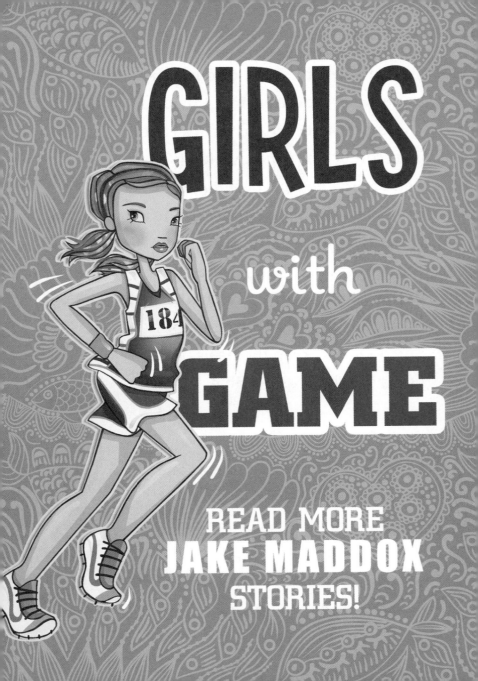

GIRLS

with

GAME

READ MORE
JAKE MADDOX
STORIES!

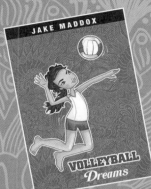

JAKE MADDOX

VOLLEYBALL
Dreams

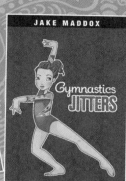

JAKE MADDOX

Gymnastics
JITTERS

JAKE MADDOX

SOCCER
SURPRISE

JAKE MADDOX

REBOUND
TIME

JAKE MADDOX

Running
SCARED

JAKE MADDOX

HORSEBACK
Hurdles

JAKE MADDOX

SKATING
Showdown

JAKE MADDOX

DANCE TEAM
DILEMMA

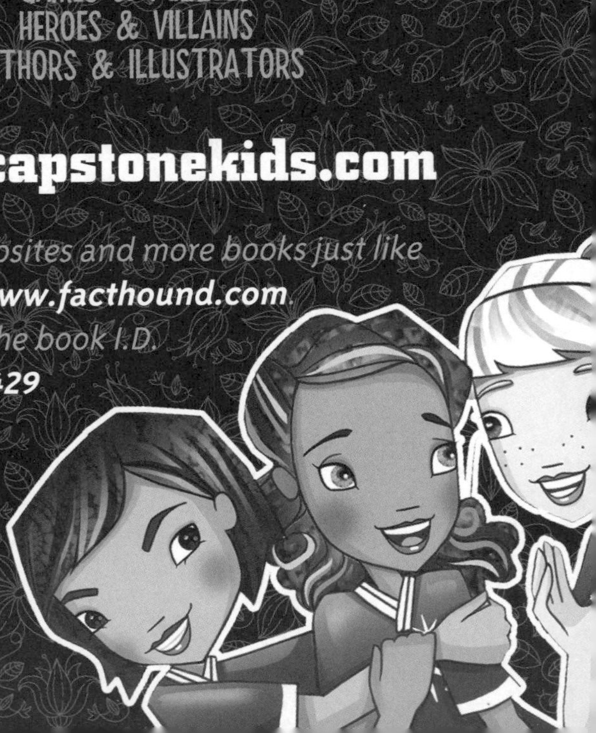